The Fatal Hour

Cover Design by: JF ANSTEAD

Xantotsu

You have come here to stand in the darkness
with me. To hear my story. You're scared.
Just write. Here I have a flask of brandy it
will insulate you from the cold. But there is
no insulation like that for the real world.
Let's start here. The word assassin is defined
by websters dictionary as a murderer, one
who carries out a plot to kill a prominent
person. The word assassin is derived from
the word hashishin. Led by Hasan Al Sabah,
the old man of the mountain, the hashishin
cult based in the fortress of Alamut in Iran
were a fearless band of political killers.
According to Marco Polo when Hasan Al
Sabah wished to kill someone he would take
a man and say. "Go do this thing. I do this
because I want you to return to paradise."

1

The Fatal Hour

And the assassins having been plied with
hashish and other pleasures would perform
the deed willingly. You wanted to meet a
real life assassin and here I am. I need to tell
my story and you need to hear it. I cannot
tell you my name. I have many names and
many passports. Lets see the readers can
know me as....ah...Nelson...Ankh. Sounds
like a super hero. My family owned a
papermill. I won't be too precise but lets just
say we lived somewhere in the united states.
I was from a young age captivated by the
culture of Japan. This led me directly to
ninjitsu. It is the martial art of the famed
ninja's of medieval Japan. They were at a
disadvantage so they created the first kind of
stealth warfare. The original teachings of
ninjitsu were developed from experiential
knowledge of combat methods and human
psychology. It is the Japanese science of
survival under any circumstance. What
captivated me most was the concept of Ki
Ai or total harmony. It is to be in touch with
the currents of nature. The pulse of the earth,
the waves of the wind, the ripples on the
lake. The fictional book about assassins by

The Fatal Hour

Trevanian talks about shibumi. It means
effortless perfection. But to the Japanese it
has to do with beauty and elegance.
Perfection. It is unattainable I believe
trevanian was reaching for the zen word
Mushin japanese for no mind. It is to be in
the moment and in the flow of nature. To not
think at all but be the moment. And when
you are in the moment you are invincible.
Shibumi means to me the act of perfecting
yourself. The very purpose of our spirit.
Each day we walk that path towards a
perfection we can never attain. Shibumi is
not in the attainment but the daily quest, the
process, of achieving your personal best.
Your perfection. You can not achieve
perfection without the Xantotsu. This is a
Japanese samurai word. It refers to archery.
It means to always strike the heart. To never
miss. Both in ethics and in action the
Xantotsu the never erring way of being is
essential. We live without forethought. We
do not guide our actions with precision. If
we did we would not make mistakes. In my
business mistakes are fatal. You must be
right the first time or you are dead. Yes it is

3

strange to hear an assassin talk about ethics but I am I believe an ethical man. I choose carefully who I kill. I created a charity to save children who were conscripted to fight wars. You think I am a bad man because I kill for money. But your soldiers do the same thing. But you say they fight for a cause. This is my craft. I am the best. It is only slightly different from warfare. My cause is the children. I was recruited into this business by an agency of the government that is too secret to even mention. They do not exist and now neither do I. They found me at a martial arts exposition. I was displaying the art of ninjitsu and they were looking for someone with my special skills. I don't know how they convinced me. I dropped out of college to pursue this carreer. They gave me a cover and they finished my training. I did that for a while but I found the private practice more lucrative. I am the most expensive assassin in the world. That is why I am the best. You'd be surprised at the market for this kind of thing.

The Fatal Hour

Governments, individuals, and even corporations. They sometimes like to kill the competition literally. But I pick and choose. I weigh the merits of the people and the outcome. I do not take any job only those that fit my own ethical standard. Almost all my money goes into the children. There are almost 250,000 children that are fighting wars. That should not be. Children should be in school. At home…But that is another thing. I will tell you my most prominent adventure. It is an opera so with each segment I will define the music that is the soundtrack to this story. All opera's like assassination always end in death.

La Donna I Mobile from Rigolleto by Verdi

It starts in a chateau somewhere in the alps. Somewhere in Europe. It is a glittering party of the elite. It is a birthday for the host. He is my target. Happy birthday. He made components for C4 or plastic explosives. His clients were governments, corporations even terrorists. My client was a European

The Fatal Hour

government I will not mention their name .I
enter through the kitchen dressed as kitchen
help. "You are late." The chef says.
I nodded. "Sorry signiori."
I said in my fake Italian accent. I began to
make my special potion. The chef looked at
me angry. "What are you doing now!" "I'm
sorry I was up late at the clubs last night. I
am making a tonic." I need you to par boil
and peel me some tomatoes, you know how
to do that?"
I nodded. "Yes signiori as soon as I finish
my tonic." Its an old recipe from ancient
Egypt. It is called asp. It is made from
simple things. It used the seeds of a fruit
which I will keep secret. It is a common
fruit. I crush the seeds. I put a quarter cup
of water in it. I put it in the microwave for 5
minutes. The intense heat expresses the
chemical I need from the seeds. I add lemon
juice and salt. It makes sodium sionide a
lethal poison. While nobody looks I dip an
expensive fountain pen's point into the
potion. I replace that in my garments that are
underneath my garments. I walk to a closet
and I take off the white kitchen smock.

6

The Fatal Hour

Underneath is a black tuxedo coat tucked in
my trousers. I had purposely worn a smock
several sizes larger to hide the bulk of my
coat. I brushed the wrinkles out of my
tuxedo. I smoothly entered the party. I was
immediately offered champagne. I made my
way through the crowd like a panther. The
ornate pen was in my pocket like an elegant
accessorie. I found my host was talking to
some guests. He was sublimely unaware that
those very people he had done business with
had wanted to clear the trail of his existence.
He was no longer in demand. He was their
suki Japanese for vulnerability.
Governments hate to be implicated in their
own naughtiness. It is the way of
democracy. It is the way of politics.
Politicians live by the public face and dabble
in the black arts the covert arts to do their
daily bidding. In truth a wise public would
insure better oversight. Wiser better would
be the seperation of the act of governing
from the act of politics. But I'm an assassin
I'm not a philosopher. I moved my way to
the balcony. Nobody was at the balcony at
that moment just me and a gardenia bush.

The Fatal Hour

The scent of the gardenia colored my simple
actions. I took out my cell phone. I opened
the back. I took out the batteries. Fishing in
pocket I took out another brand of battery.
Any one who reads the battery instructions
knows that there is a danger of explosion if
the battery is incorrectly replaced. But to do
it right you have to test and test until you
know which batteries go boom and how
quickly. I turned the cell phone power on
and put it in the gardenia bush. I walked
sleekly back into the party. I moved toward
my host. He was smiling and laughing. His
back was to me. I looked at my watch.
Suddenly there was an explosion on the
balcony. The crowd turned as they heard the
bang!! As they did I struck the host on the
back of the neck with the poisoned pen. He
grabbed his neck. Looked at his hand. I
replaced the poison pen elegantly into my
coat pocket. He moved toward the balcony.
He was already dizzy. He took two steps and
fainted. He would never wake up from his
birthday slumber. I made my way to the
door. I handed my glass of champagne to the

butler as I left. "Goodnight sir will you not stay for the gifts."

I smiled. "My gift is there already but you know business before pleasure. Goodnight." I walked out the door and a limousine was waiting for me. I stepped in. The chauffer closed the door. We slowly drove away from the chateau. I took out another cell phone and dialed a number. "Hello this is Mr. Black your little troubles have been erased. I expect the final payment to be delivered to the charity. Yes the war children's fund. Thank you. Pleasure doing business with you." I rolled down the window and threw the cell phone out into the darkness. My job done I headed home to Valhalla.

Un Bel Di from Madama Butterfly by Puccini

Promises of paradise are a common human thread. In Nordic reference Valhalla is the place where heroes go to rest after death. It is a feast where wine is plentiful and men of courage exchange stories and enjoy the pleasures of the afterlife. It is no different

than the muslim paradise promised by Al
Sabah to the hashishin. My pleasure palace
was an italian pallazo that sat on the
foothills of mount erebus in the Caucasus.
A place of high grasslands, wild flowers and
rolling mountains. Geoligists call this part of
the mare imbrium or its eastern lip. A point
between the Caspian and black seas that
joins Europe to asia. With cliff's that drop
more than a mile the Caucasus are one of the
worlds most challenging terrains. That is
why I chose it as my home. The interior of
my palazzo was decorated in the
quintessence of western heritage. My love of
renaissance painters, medieval curtains, and
Persian rugs was obvious. I was one of
Sotheby's most exclusive and anonymous
customers. Intermixed with the western was
the oriental. Swords, silk, masks and large
vases. It was the most sumptuous of retreats.
Like most itallian palazzo's it had a
courtyard. This I made into the most perfect
Japanese garden of round rocks, bonsai,
cherry trees, ponds of coy fish and running
streams. It was serenity. It was the moon on
the water. A zen sword term that describes

The Fatal Hour

how to attain the greatest invincibility. The greatest tranquility. The greatest connection to the flow of nature that is the very windmill in your soul. Your innersight. Your nirvana.

My live in companion was a Japanese geisha named Sabi. Sabi is Japanese for tranquility and inner peace. A geisha is a work of art. From her painted face to her perfect grace. From her silk kimono to her laquered hair pins. She was the very emanation of the muses in an eastern form. The word geisha means literally arts person. She is trained from a young age in the traditional arts of japan. Music, dancing, flower arranging and many many more things. Geisha are not prostitutes. Though they were often found in brothels they were there to perform art not to sell their bodies. They cultivated an aesthetic understated form of feminine sexiness. Not submissive as westerners think. It is called iki. It is an elegance that intrigues, an alluring style that reflects the whole philosophy of Japanese life. Though the geisha were meant to be pure as cherry blossoms they could take a lover. I am her

11

danna or patron. Sabi is beauty by virtue of her very soul. She cooks traditional Japanese meals. Miso, udon, soba. My favorite is chirashi which is vinagered rice topped with raw fish. She makes me rosebuds of tuna sashimi. Before dinner she will dance and sing with her silk fan. While I eat she will play the shamisen a 3 stringed instument. Then while she eats I do a flower arrangement for her that she taught me how to do. She smiles demurely lays her long neck to one side. Ours is a spiritual exchange. The approach to the palazzo is guarded by a shepherd named Balkin. He is a noxche the indigenous people of the Caucasus. They live in rugged stone villages built high atop mountains with small footpaths as the only entrance. These are called auols and they are the place of a teip or a clan. The noxche are nature worshippers they have been influenced by other religions but their native form of pantheism similar to Shinto is the living spirit of their land. Balkin often tells me. "We noxche are the grass on the mountain we clump in our aouls and we are defined by our teips but we never change. We have existed for thousands of years unchanged. When the wind blows muslim, when the wind blows Christian or even Soviet we like the grass bend in the wind but never break. We will be here forever as long as clouds bloom and mountains dare scratch the sky with their claws." Then he would always look at me with those black eyes. "I am a shepherd you are a wolf. We are friends. As long as you do not steal my sheep and instead consume my neighbors flock. I am not only grateful but I grow stronger." It is very Russian but also the essence of noxche. Sabi calls me by the nickname Wabi. Wabi means poverty in Japanese. But it means more. To be poor is not to be dependent on worldly things. To feel inwardly the presence of something of the highest value without need for fame, wealth or power. In a sense wabi and sabi are opposites. Westerners know wabi sabi as the beautiful ugly. Sabi is beautiful and wabi is ugly. But in one sense wabi and sabi are interchangeable and denote how external emptiness is filled by inner richness. Our relationship is of that nature. Our external appearances are perceived as cool but our passions boil deep. Making love is our greatest discipline. It is the exchange between our spirits. The very connection of our souls. For the Geihsa making love is a formal engagement it is an evocation of tradition. She would sit there before me on a persian rug in front of our bed. I would sit on the opposite side looking at her. Before us was a bowl of water and a sea sponge. She was dressed in a red silk kimono with images of a Japanese pillow book that told the tale of lovers throughout her gown. Everytime we made love she was the bride of the night and as the betrothed we must honor each other with our feelings in poetry. I as the man I spoke first beseeching her love. "A moth's wings kissed the sky. It was not the only kiss. But the first kiss of spring. Winter is my blanket until the flood. Until the rain. Until every stream stretches its hand to the sea." She wielded her iki mercilessly. She smiled. Looked down at the rug. Then up at my eyes.I felt her inner joy. Then she said. "The cherry was sour. The wind sweet. The blossoms like rain. Every

stream has its purpose. My purpose is to
catch blossoms. Soft like the moss. A
butterfly in my hand. The memory of
snowflakes on my lips." I smiled. She
leaned her neck to one side. And I knew she
could feel my inner joy. Then with a soft
precision as if in a ritual she began to wipe
her white paint off her face. It was
seduction. Every wipe revealed her flesh. It
was soft it was warm and it yearned to be
touched. Each revelation opened a door to
her soul. Finally she wiped her painted lips
but in such a way that I felt my lips on hers.
With each touch of sponge I felt my passion
well in my nether regions. Her iki was
supreme. She was the daughter of a long line
of geisha. It is one way you enter the
sisterhood of art. But before her ancestors
were Geisha they were Oiran. Oiran were
great court ladies. They were the highest
form of Japanese courtesan. They were
termed castle destroyers because their sex
appeal like the mythical beauties in history
could destroy a man as easily as an army.
But the oiran vanished into the mist of
Japanese history like the samurai. Once they

were gone only the geisha remained. So the oiran traditions were kept by families and passed mother to daughter. They were the secret. The power of woman veiled in the guise of pure and demurre geisha dolls. Only through a secret society called "waterworld" could you access these special beauties. It was a gift from the Emperor of japan. She pulled the laquered pins from her hair and it fell like the gates of Tokyo. She was suddenly worldly like deep wild forests open like Mount Fuji to the sky. She unwrapped her obi which was a cloth that wound round her waist. As she released the tension of her kimono it opened slowly revealing first the oncoming slopes of her round breasts then the soft supple skin that reached down toward her navel. She stood and I walked forward. She looked in my eyes her lips puffed and open like an orchid. I moved my hands into her kimono. I stroked her body. She leaned back and I kissed her throat. I picked her up in my arms and carried her to the big bed that had gauze curtains and silk sheets. The wind blew the gauze round her body and as her kimono fell to the

The Fatal Hour

ground I could see a veiled glance at her
erect nipples. There on the bed was a
dessicated tube of sea cucumber that Sabi
had rehydrated and lay on the silk sheets. It
is an oiran secret she placed it over my penis
and it was meant to be the organic version of
a French tickler. Her pubic hair was shaved
and her rosebud was like a deep tropical
flower. The carnivorous kind with sweet
juices that digest the very soul. We chose
the horse position.
She is the furious rider and I am the fast
horse. As I entered her honeyed realm I
could feel two little balls roll on the side of
my erection. As we started to move the balls
would chime. As she rode my skin the balls
would ring like bridle of a horse. The gauze
curtains blew in the wind and she caught
them and wrapped them round her face and
breasts. I kissed her nipples through the
gauze. The veil guarded her mouth as she
breathed in my lips. I grabbed her hips and
pulled her onto my hardness. She rode me
with great pleasure. Creating a poem as she
rode a sexual poem.

The Fatal Hour

"The long reed pierces the water and the ripples flow out to the lip of the lake. I feel it like the moon. Yearning for more ripples. Yearning for the deepest reed. The moon quenches its thirst by licking the lake. But the reed is so deep. It is deeper than the moon as it touches my waters. The open flowers of my spring… oh….oh don't stop Wabi." We men have also our secrets. The patience of a hunter that must wait for his prey. Stopping builds her senses by its emptiness. The power of zen is the emptiness that fills your soul. "Oh please wabi..please wabi." She bent over and her lips gently touched mine. The greatest secret of the Oiran is the seppun. It is a kiss it is a concentual rape of the mouth. She inserted her toungue. I inserted my tongue. We repeated the volleys. Like great frigates we broadsided each others mouth. The seppun is ecstacy. She wailed at first softy. Then with all her soul like a monk at Buddhist prayer. Then she screamed releasing the chi in her loins. Like a bear in a trap I groaned. My lictor spilled through the sea cucumber and mixed with her sweet nectars. It was as

18

The Fatal Hour

our souls like sugar and water mixed and becoming one. The sweetness of our spirit one flower dripping in the dews of our erotic engagement. I felt her breathe and with each breath I felt part of what she was and she felt my heart and with each beat she understood my inner essence. This is how we lived. In pleasure. In true serenity. In our own special nirvana.

Vesti La Giuba from Pagliacci by Leoncavallo

How do you hire a professional assassin? Well you go through a death broker. You've probably never heard of death brokers. They act like agents for assassins. My broker is the Creative Artist Agency of the assassination business. We call him Dr. Death. His name is Mohamed bin Salam. He is a Javanese. His offices are in a glass tower he built in Jakarta Indonesia. He is a Medical Doctor and also a muslim cleric and also a pirate and most especially a death broker. His tower is devoted to some legitimate business but mostly the business

19

of assassination. It is a flourishing market. There is an assassin for every type of situation. Some more or less amateurish some precision engineering like me. He makes connections between the buyer and the seller. His clients are almost universal from angry husbands to drug cartels to foreign governments. Every one it seems wants to kill someone. And he is more than happy to profit from it. In order to reach me he must send a courier to the Russian republic Kabardino-Balkaria and visit the city of Tyrnyauz staying at the Savoy hotel. Here the courier will leave a message with front desk for Mr. Green. I rent anonymously a room at the Savoy just for this message purpose. Every couple of days Balkin will visit Tyrnyauz driving my black hummer H2 and picking up any messages at the Savoy and often taking his wife shopping. This time I received a message not very long after my last job at the chateau. So as always I made my pilgrimage to Jakarta to visit Dr. Death. On arriving I would make a call and say to him the words from Omar Kayam's Rubiyat "I sometimes think that never blows so red the rose as where some buried ceasar bled." He would hang up and meet me in a small café and sip mint tea as we talked of death. He often quoted the Koran. "The angel of death who is given charge of you shall cause you to die." I replied. "Then your lord you shall be brought back." He laughed. "You know the Koran so well you could be a muslim." I smiled. "Like god I am many things to many people."

"You still live with the painted woman in your paradise on the mountain."

Quoting the Koran I said. "It is in the Inevitable. 'So he shall seek a life of pleasure."

He replied. "It is in the Night. 'Except the seeking of pleasure of the lord the most high." I picked up the folder he had laid in front of me. "The CIA is it?"

"They need you to put a lost sheep to sleep."

Quoting the Rubiyat I said "Some for the glories of this world; and some sigh for the prophet's paradise to come; ah, take the cash, and let the credit go." I closed the file and said. "So even terrorists are turning agents into double agents." Then I smiled. "They have their price we have ours." "The CIA is notoriously cheap about these things but they will pay our price." While I thought he quoted the Koran. "The love of desires of women and hoarded treasures of gold and silver and well bred horses and cattle and tilth is made to seem fair to men, this is the provision of life in this world, and Allah is with whom is the good goal of life." I finished my mint tea.

"Were you witness when death visited yahoub, when he said to his sons who will you serve."

He answered. "They said we will serve god and the god of your fathers, Ibrahim and Ishmael and Ishaq, one god only and to him we submit." He finished his tea and said. "Then you will do it?"

I smiled. "Tell the CIA they will prepare a meeting between this man and me. I shall pose as his new station chief Brad Johnson. Write that down. They will make the first payment to my Seychelle Islands account. I

The Fatal Hour

will contact them for my final payment on completion of the business."

He said as we parted as always. "Tamam." I nodded and left. Tamam is Aramaic it is from the bible it means completeness it means perfection.

I was to meet my target in Paris on a bridge over the seine. It was pouring rain that night. Our meeting was for 3 A.M.. The magic hour for the dark ops. I was wearing a black trench coat. I saw him waiting there on the centermost point of the bridge. I put my garrote wire into my hand. I approached. He was looking out over the seine. Then he turned to look at me smiling like some demon. I felt a presence. I looked around me. I heard three pops of a silenced sniper rifle. Blood oozed from my chest. I fell to the ground. My target laughed. "You duds never learn. You don't kill the wrong people. Friends of The Contract will be avenged. Now you are dead. We are the power in this world not little scum bags like you." As he said this he lifted me up over the rail and dropped me into the cold seine. I felt my life oozing from my open wounds. I lay there in the water. I was dieing and I knew it. The emptiness is before me I thought no the emptiness is in me. The clouds were breaking and the moon showed its face. It glimmered on the waters. It was the beauty of utter tranquility. The moment of utter emptiness that filled my soul with life. I made my way to the shore. I lifted myself out of the water. I was shivering. I stood straight and made my way to the train station. I dialed my cell phone. Sabi answered. "I am wounded badly Sabi I need you to call the hospital at Tyrnyauz and get our doctor to meet me at Valhalla." "Why can you not get a doctor there?" She said crying. "Because that would create too many questions I can not answer." "What if you die on the way." "It is my only road. It is karma." She did not answer. She hung up. But I knew it was her way of saying come home don't die I love you. The train ride to Munich was long. I had to walk to the bathroom several times and apply paper towels to my three wounds. Once in Munich I transferred to the airport and caught Siberia Airlines flight to Mineralnie

The Fatal Hour

Vodie airport in the Russian republic of
Stavopolski Krai. During the flight my face
turned pale and I began to shiver
uncontrollabley. I was going into shock. But
the moon on the water. The emptiness of
existence it kept me aware and in control. I
rented a van and tried to dial my cell phone.
It was so difficult. But my concentration my
discipline cut through the fog of death. I
called Sabi and told her to have Balkin pick
me up at the mountain entrance in 4 hours.
The driver looked at me. "Are you alright."
"I have ulcers I'm sorry." I said. He nodded.
He left me in the middle of nowhere within
sight of the approach to mount erebus.
Suddenly head lights approached. My
Hummer drove up. Balkin caught me as I
fainted.
The doctor was waiting. He extracted the
bullets. He did all he could. I saw tears
falling down the white mask of my beautiful
Sabi. The doctor said. "He has lost too much
blood. He needs more work." He shook his
head. "I'm sorry." Balkin looked at Sabi.
"There once was a mountain and he was just
standing there touching the sky when he felt

a wind approach. The wind was the breath of death. The mountain decided to trick the wind, so he showed only stone and snow no flowers or grass. Death always seeks itself like life seeks itself. So the wind looked at this and said 'Were it not for the snow that lay there cold and frozen one might say the mountain was murdered by the sky; were it not for the hard stone one might say the mountain is just a skeleton and has died of starvation. If it was not murdered and it did not die of hunger then that means the mountain lives. So the wind passed on and the mountain was spared from death."

Sabi wiped her tears and hugged Balkin. "Will Wabi really live."

"He will not die he is filled with such great yah."

Sabi asked. "What is yah?"

"We noxche were born with cheese in one hand and iron in the other. The cheese is hospitality. The iron is strength. It is the essence of Yah. May no mother bear a child without yah. Men with yah do not die easily like the mountain they find a way to live."

The Fatal Hour

Love Duet from Madama Butterfly by Puccini

To the Japanese the chanoyu or tea ceremony transcends life and death and all worldly things. There I lay in the darkness of my wounds while Sabi performed the tea ritual. It was as if the spirit of the tea ceremony had come to blow on the embers of my dieing soul. For the very spirit of life is the ceremony. It is reverence, purity, harmony and tranquility. To the buddhist these are the only components that build our lifes architecture. These are life and yet it is all beyond life. It is all beyond death. It is the everything and nothing that makes life and death possible. Sabi began by building a universe. It was a flower arrangement only. But there is no only in zen. The ikebana means flowers kept alive. Sabi was tending my flame keeping me alive. This act of beauty and simplicity was my only connection to the thread of life. The aesthetic is the spiritual. The spirit is my very animating principle. Without the simplicity and beauty there is no life only

the completeness of death. In zen you
contemplate the universe. You do this
through ikebana, bonsai and a zen garden.
The universe is first and essential. Without it
we can not exist.
After finishing the flower arrangement Sabi
lit a brazier. It is the flame of life. The
hearth that brings us home. This was not the
standard tea ceremony. That would be in a
tea house which we had in our garden. But
Sabi brought the tea house to me. The
brazier was to boil the water for the tea. She
lay a bowl by her knees. The bowl she
wiped clean with a cloth. Then folded the
cloth. Then with the same cloth she wiped a
spoon and then refolded the cloth. She then
took the ladle and poured the water into the
bowl. But then she throws the water into
another container and wipes the bowl clean
again. Then she takes the spoon and scoops
a measure of green tea which is a powder
into the bowl. She draws water with the
ladle into the bowl. Then she takes a
bamboo whisk and mixes the green tea.
With her right hand she turns the cup
clockwise once then twice. Then the tea is

The Fatal Hour

ready to drink. The maker of the tea must accomplish a spiritual poverty that is essential to the tea ceremony. True poverty of spirit requires that man shall be emptied of god and all his works, so that if god wants to act in the soul he can. Therefore the ultimate goal of the tea ceremony is to empty our souls so that god may fill them. The morning sun shown through the veil of curtains and god filled my soul. I felt life returning. But I was as fragile as a newborn butterfly. Wabi touched my bandages and I grabbed her hand. She looked in my eyes. I had not spoken in many weeks so my throat was dry. "Sabi I have been thinking. I have been your danna for many years are you happy here."

Sabi smiled. "Happiness is wind across water. But joy is the earth under my feet." I said. "Sabi I no longer want you as a bride for a single night. But as the bride of my day and the bride of my night for as long as I may breath."

Sabi looked down. Then at the love in my eyes. "I would no longer be a sister of art." "You would be a mother of art." She hugged

me. "We are two winds that meet on a
mountain. I pass through you. You pass
through me."
"I love you Sabi. Be my wife." She nodded
and began to cry. Sabi took the laquered
pins from her hair. "I am betrothed I am no
longer a sister I am the chrysalis of a wife."
She would never dress as a geisha again.
She now took the role of wife to be. Her
face was no longer painted. But her art
remained a central part of her life and mine.
The aesthetic does not go away only the veil
of purity. As I grew stronger she brought me
shaniken or throwing stars and I threw them
at a target from my bed. Soon I was walking
slowly. I would need lots of reststops but I
could make my way to the dinner table.
There she would join me and we would sit
and talk. Then after dinner she would play
the shamisen and sing. She was so happy
she seemed to glow. I soon was strong
enough to begin doing tai chi and sabi would
join me and in our slow ballet like the wind
through the valley. Tai chi is a slow
movement that not only strengthens the
muscle but nourishes the soul. In the

emptiness was the wind and the trees. The trees were cast about by the wind and this did not break the trees but made them stronger. Tai chi is the precursor to kung fu. It is the movement of life that is the very protection from harm. It is the way of everything. Everything has harmony. And in harmony there is a balance. The ability to heal is balanced by the ability to harm. We are the eye that is the focus between tai chi and kung fu. The scales fall and rise with our choices with our life.

Kung fu is one part of ninjitsu. For the purpose of ninjitsu is to learn many arts and bind them together as one. For each ninja it is different. For me it was sword, kung fu, aikido and judo. These were my roots but the tree in ninjitsu grows its own way and according to its own needs. No ninja fights the same. We are all the manifestation of our creativity and the inspiration that lay in the roots we chose. Soon I was hiking up the mountain passes of erebus with balkin. This was always an act of aesthetic pleasure and exercise. I was growing stronger and with my strength came a thirst for revenge. Who

The Fatal Hour

was The Contract and why did they do this
to me. It was obvious I had killed someone
they thought worthy of avenging. But
vengeance always breeds vengeance. It was
clear the CIA was involved in my
assassination. But why? I needed to
meditate.
I sat in the lotus position in my Japanese
garden. The garden was the universe. It was
the universe and I alone. I felt the cool
Caucasus breeze on my face. I closed my
eyes. I thought cold..cold…colder. I felt a
shiver down my spine. I am a snowbird. The
ground and the sky are white. Snowflakes
are falling on the cherry trees. Only the
bones of winter reach out from the snow.
Using my wings I rise up to the sky. From
low altitude it is all white and gray like a
Japanese watercolour. I go higher and I see
the purple and brown mountain slopes. The
clouds pass me white like the snow and I
rise higher. Now I can view the sea washing
our shores in the distance. Then I go higher I
see the blue and red sprites the very sparks
of the ionosphere. With easy strength I make
my way into planetary orbit. I can see the

The Fatal Hour

blue orb filled with continents and turquoise seas. Now with my last strength I fly to the sun. Hot… hot…hotter. I feel the sweat on my brow. The sun is an open doorway in the universe. I fly into its eye. Then I am here in my garden again. My journey was to me. For I am the beginning and the end of all journeys. I open my eyes. I know what to do.
With my building strength I now planned my return to the world of living. I filled a pack with 50 pound weights and ran through the causasus landscapes. Balkin drove behind me in the hummer. Mount erebus framed our every action. The purpose of bonsai is to construct a miniature universe of balance and harmony. It must be tended. It is like tending your family. Guiding your children. Minding your home. As you cut away with pruning shears you cut away that of the universe that no longer is in harmony. Each bonsai has its inner truth. This is the essence of truth. This truth is true for only this one bonsai. We cut away all the falseness in life that surrounds the truth and if you do it right you are always left with the

inner tree the true truth. As bonsai tenders
we are keepers of the truth and we seek it for
it is inside us as it is inside the tree.
What is The Contract. I did not know. So I
began my surveillance. I needed to develop
intelligence on this entity if I was to seek my
revenge. What is revenge but the putting of
harmony back into your life. The return of
the tranquility of your soul. I have worked
on the problems of surveillance with the
discipline of an eastern mind and the
intellect of a western mind. I have developed
many new tools. From an intricate network
of computers called the nautilus to a wavelet
detecting device they are the children of
necessity. The nautilus is a computer that
operates a computer that operates a
computer and on and on 100 fold. It is a
network but quite different from the
expected. One controls the next and I have
control of what is called chamber one.
Chamber one only controls chamber two and
so on up the chain. The network is
distributed all over the world. The purpose
of nautilus is to evade detection and
maximize control. The available memory for

any application is upwards of a terabyte.
You can not detect it and it can control
multiple junctions. Say you want to control
the phone switches in the worldwide phone
system. You use nautilus to capture and
control. That is what I did. All I had to do is
call my former CIA contact. The one I made
through doctor death. The phone answered.
"Phillip stern."
I said. "Yes Mr. Stern I am trying to reach
The Contract."
"Never heard of it."
I smiled. "Well thank you anyway." I hung
up. He hung up. Then he picked up again.
The phone dialed. It was a Baltimore
Maryland number. The phone answered.
"John Wright."
"Yeah John I just received a call from a
man asking about The Contract. Someone
has sprung a leak. Heads up."
"I will inform Mr. Evans immediately." I
followed the chain of calls. "Yes." "There is
a leak somewhere."
"Get your best people on it. They must not
follow the trail of The Contract here.
Extreme measures are the ROE. Get to it."

The Fatal Hour

"Yes sir."
The trail led directly to The Vector
Corporation. It was a defense contractor. It
had contracts to design airplanes for the Air
Force, submarines for the Navy, lasers for
the Army, and surveillance technology for
the Intelligence community. At least that is
what was public knowledge. The more I
uncovered the more I discovered something
more sinister. I rented a room at a hotel
across the street from the Vector corporation
in Baltimore. I set up my surveillance center
there. I used my wavelet detector. It is a
machine that detects waves only of light,
sound, all energy. It does this by emmiting
radiowaves that are focused into a beam.
The beam disturbs the environment with a
specific frequency and amplitude. This
causes the other waves that make up
everything else to interfere with the radio
waves. This gives off an interference pattern
that is picked up by my machines radio
detector. This is the wave signal properties
that permeate all environments. It is quite
unique. A wavelet is the fundamental
principle of the wave in nature. It is never a

The Fatal Hour

particle. It is always a wave. It is nothing
and everything. My laptop computer
detailed the incoming data for me. I listened
to them all and I learned quite a bit about
The Contract.

The Contract is the ultimate military
contractor. It is a secret deal between the
U.S. government and Vector Corp. It is
worth nearly $300 billion and makes Vector
the exclusive contractor for the CIA, NSA,
FBI and DOD. This would allow for
streamlining of the national security
apparatus that had lacked cohesion before
9/11. It was noble to tear down the curtain
between departments but this meant that the
entire security of the United States depended
upon the integrity of one private contractor.
Something neither congress or the public
could accept. So instead of taking a political
hit. The President made The Contract the
deepest national secret possible. Nobody
was to know. This made Allford Evans the
Chairman and CEO of Vector the most
powerful man in the world. But what was
the connection between the man in the
chateau and The Contract. Apparently

37

The Fatal Hour

Allford's sister is married to the man in the chateau. So without realizing it I had assassinated the brother in law of a very dangerous and powerful man. I prepared my next step very carefully.

Non Pui Andrai, Farfallone Amoroso from Le Nozze di Figaro by Mozart

The assassination attempt on me was a wake up call. The awakening is central to zen. It is the abrupt realization of the truth of zen. A monk asks his master. 'What is the Budha'. The master answers. 'The Budha'. The monks asks again.'What is zen." The master answers. 'Zen." What is is. This is the the final fact the completeness of experience. I needed to enter the building and penetrate its deepest places without raising alarm. I needed to get my passive electromagnetic sensors in front of the security system that raised the electronic fence around the building. So I became Dr. David Brown. What is is. I was dead. So they did not expect me to appear any time soon. And certainly not walk through their

38

front door. The advantage was mine. I first had to develop the snare. The laboratory studying wavelets. I submitted papers to DARPA. They worked for Vector so quickly Mr. Evans heard about my research and was intrigued. I was invited to meet the powerful Allford Evans and I was enchanted at the opportunity. I taped the sensors to my waist and adjusted the digital camera in my jacket button. I was ready to enter the dragons lair and get a deeper appreciation of their security mechanisms. Everywhere I walked my sensors mapped the electrical frequencies. This would describe all the hidden sensors that were there when the doors closed. I entered the office of Mr. Evans and promptly introduced myself to his assistant. She said "Mr. Evans is waiting for you." So I went right in. Allford Evans was an older man in his sixties. His hair was thinning but he had the posture of a king. His handshake was a challenge and as I was only a scientist I let him win.

"I've heard good things about you Dr. Brown. Please sit down. And can we get you some coffee. I grow these coffee beans on a farm I have in Kenya. I have a special furnace process that roasts the beans to a deep super espresso. It is unique. We also are working on a genetic merging of the coffee bean and guarana plants. This would make super caffeinated beans that we can use for keeping the troops awake. But you know everything is interesting to me….especially if it has national security applications." I was given a mug of coffee. I looked at Mr. Evans.

"My research is very special to me I have spent a long time developing the techniques I use."

Mr. Evans smiled. "Its very special to us too." I touched my button and unbuttoned my coat. The digital camera captured a view of his personal computer. That is the mcguffin the thing that will drive Mr. Evans to make a deal. A deal would allow both of us to operate as equals.It would be sufficient revenge to have the goods on Mr. Evans. The computer contains all the e-mail messages he makes with all his people. All I have to do is acquire it.

The Fatal Hour

Mr. Evans looked at me and said. "I have read your descriptions of the wavelet it reminds me of the Holy spirit. Are you a religious man Dr. Brown."
I quoted the bible. "Create me in a clean heart, O god; and renew a right spirit within me. Cast me not away from thy presence; and take not thy holy spirit from me."
Mr. Evans grinned from ear to ear. "Psalm 51." I nodded. "So many scientists I talk to are such humanists. They are not men of faith like you and I. I want to talk to you more. Maybe you could visit my church." Said Mr. Evans "I would enjoy that." I said. Mr. Evans like many people was truly a man of faith. But it was redemption that was his necessity for religion. The idea of salvation for all sins no matter what you have done is very attractive to men like Mr. Evans. They use it to wipe their hands clean from all the dirt. "Christ be with you." He said as I left his office. I got across the street and I dumped the data from sensors and camera onto my laptop. I studied the security layout and developed a plan. Lao Tzu said attack when least expected. Soon I would strike.

Mattinata by Leoncavallo

There are five security measures you can put in a building. The first is visual. Infrared cameras that see through the darkness. Second is the basic motion or thermal sensor. This see's without eyes the changes in temperature in a room. Third is seismic sensors that literally pick up any motions on the ground. Fourth is a passive door sensor that notices when a door is ajar. It is no different than the clay put on doors by the Sumerians 3000 years ago. The fifth are laser optic sensors that are invisble to the eye and once blocked set off all the alarms. They are the most challenging. Beating all these is the occupation of the modern day ninja. I studied the security service that worked for the building. There had been an opening. So I applied. My first day was not long after my visit to Mr. Evans. I was on the skeleton crew. The night shift. Midnight to 7 AM. It gave me access to enter the building without suspicion. Without the cameras noticing my entrance. I was just one

of the security crew. Everyday that I
worked I brought a back pack with my
snacks and some music. I worked for several
weeks. This allowed me to develop a normal
routine. Everything was as expected. Time
to strike.
The master says. 'Do you see the flower.'
The monk says.'I am the flower." This is
how mushin must be. To be in no mind is to
experience only. It is to not see but be. I am
not a swordsman I am only a sword. Thus is
the preparation for action in my mind. I put
my palms together breath in the emptiness.
Exhale the suchness. I am then ready for
action.
The cameras are not everywhere. They are
used to guard all entrances. The entrances
also had the passive door sensors so I was
already passed two of the five security
measures in the building. Once inside the
cameras all disappear. Therefore all I had to
do is go on my rounds through the building.
I entered an office and discarded my clothes.
I was carrying my backpack because as was
my routine I would stop somewhere for a
snack and while I walked I would play my

music. I opened the zipper wide on the
backpack and inside was a ninja sword. The
sword is the ninja-to it is a short blade and
straight not curved like a samurai sword.
The sword to the ninja is not his soul. His
soul is nature. He is the child of the wind.
The sword is the storm. Inside the backpack
was another backpack all black. I put the
sword on my back. Then I put the back pack
over it. The sword handle lay ready over my
shoulder. I was all in ninja black. I moved
quietly through the building. My first
obstacle was the motion sensor. These are
calibrated to reach 1 foot above the floor. So
I took off my backpack and lay on my back.
I moved the backpack with me as I myself
moved. It was a careful exercise. But I was
soon past the sensor and deeper into the
buildings more secure areas. Each area is
secured according to its level of
confidentiality. The area where the guards
walk are non confidential, the area secured
by the motion sensor is confidential, the area
secured by the seismic sensors is secret, the
area secured by lasers is the pinnacle the
final top secret. I moved through the

confidential areas and entered the secret area that was secured by a closed locked door. The only access is a card. I pulled out of my backpack a small hand held computer and I opened up the card reader. It used a magetic stripe to read a code. So once I had the wires connected. I downloaded a series of numbers from a random number generator. This took a moment but soon the door clicked open. The same technique can be used to access ATM's but I am an assassin not a thief. There before me was a floor that was connected to a seismograph and if the movement reaches a threshold limit the seismograph will turn all the alarms on. The seismic sensor covered the ground in the hallway. So I pulled out of my backpack what was basically a nail driver that has a high tension wire connected to the nail spike it spits out. I shot it across the room and it nailed in the arch of the distant doorway. I unhooked the wire and replaced it on a new spike. I closed a clip on the wire end and loaded the spike into the nail gun. I shot it up close at the archway above me. Now there was a wire that stretched across the hallway. I put on gloves and pulled out two hooks. Using the hooks I climbed hand over hand across the wire suspended over the floor. I was very careful and I made it through without trouble.

I made my way through the secret areas and I took the elevator in this secret section to a 8th floor office. The building had 20 floors. It was the office of Allford Evans. I took out a can of spray. It is a mister it is used to detect the presence of infrared lasers. I turned on the mister. And it layed a fog in the room. Soon you could see the rays of laser beams that like splinters from the ceiling blocked my path. With carefull almost tai chi motions I made my way through the forrest of lasers. It took me five minutes and then I was in. There before me was Mr. Evan's computer. I opened the computer tower. I unhooked the C drive and as I did the buiding's alarm went off. Soon a security team would be on me.

Ancient ninja knew that you always prepare an escape plan or you prepare to die.

The Fatal Hour

Champagne Aria from Don Giovanni by Mozart

Lao Tzu's Art of War is the bible of the
ninja. It defines how we act in the world. In
this case I was reminded that to achieve a
withdrawl that can not be stopped depart
with superior speed. So I headed for the
emergency stair case. As I moved I lay small
tape recorders that fit in the palm of your
hand. I lay them at strategic spots. I heard a
helicopter land on the roof. I was going just
that direction. They were smart they wanted
to trap me between their men from below
and their men from above. I took out a credit
card sized remote control. I hit the on.
Suddenly you heard shooting. They were
firing back at a ghost. I was not there. As
Lao Tzu put it if they are substantial prepare
for them, if they are strong avoid them. Now
I only had the people on the roof to contend
with. I reached the roof door before they did.
I heard them approaching. As they opened
the door I pushed. The first man there I
kicked in the head. The second man I Threw
a shaniken and struck his throat. The third

man was farther away. He lifted his automatic weapon. The ancient ninjas swords were made inferior to the samurai swords. They were meant for stabbing mostly not sword fighting. But I did not have the disadvantage of being a ninja peasant so I made my sword of high quality carbon steel. The man aimed his rifle at me. Lao Tzu said if near appear far and if far appear near. I ran forward at him and tumbled on the ground. This meant he lost sight of his target. But I in one motion tumbled to my feet. My sword drew. In one single motion I cut off his hands and the rifle split in two. With my second motion I cut off his head. Then I moved to a large microwave antenna. I climbed the ladder to the top. Those that I had slowed down soon made it to the roof. I began opening telescoping tubes of steel and putting them together. I had used a rappelling clip to hook myself to the antenna. The men below began to shoot at me. I rapidly unfolded a nylon canvas. Soon the men sent someone up the ladder after me. I hooked it all together. It was a portable hand glider. I laughed as I

The Fatal Hour

unhooked and leapt out into the darkness.
My escape was complete.

**Trio: Soave Sia Il Vento from Cosi Fan
Tutte by Mozart**

The wind carried my soul. I was on my way
home. I flew through the buildings. The
lights of the city all below and bright. I flew
slowly and beautifully. Like a great soaring
bird I chased the wind. The wind was my
friend. I was its child. I was free to marry
my sweet sabi. As I flew I began to compose
my wedding poem. "In winter I find warm
residence in your eyes. In spring your lips
are the rivers that flow from mountain to sea
from you to me. Summer is the land of duty
and honor and industry. I work for your sake
you work for mine. Autumn is the end and
in the end as in the beginning my home is
with you and beside you...." It was a work
in progress. I thought it ironic that on her
wedding day sabi would be again in white
paint as the bride must visibly show purity
in her maidenhood to the gods. Weddings
are primarily a Shinto ceremony in Japan.

49

Our wedding vows are poems. We dress in beautiful kimonos. She wears an ornate head piece for luck. Central to the ceremony is the drinking of nine cups of sake. After which the couple is married. Every ounce of my being awaited that day with the deepest yearning.

Un Bel Di from Madama Butterfly by Puccini (Reprise)

I arrived at the Mineralnie Vodie Airport 2 days later. I rented a van and the driver took me to the mountain entrance to erebus. I did not have Balkin pick me up in the hummer. Instead I walked. This was to insure nobody followed me or could follow me in the future to my Valhalla. My home in the hills. As I looked at the Caucasus mountain range before me it reminded me of the old lady of the mountain in Japanese tradition. In Japanese her name is yamauba and she represents the principle of love that secretly moves in every one of us. This is because

The Fatal Hour

love is such a tremendous labour that it
makes the spirit of love white haired and
wrinkled from all the difficulties. Yamauba
brings people together for the rest of their
lives. She also in a sense represents the idea
that death which is also old and wrinkled is
much the same as love. We can not know
true love without knowing death. For it is in
the loss. The death. That we realize the true
meaning and value of love. I was making
my way to Valhalla. I could could see my
palazzo just over the next hill. Suddenly I
heard a low roar. I could not make it out for
a moment. But soon I heard the distinct
sound of helicopters in the distance. I started
to move a little faster. Then I saw them clear
like hawks on the horizon two black apache
helicopters. I began to run. I screamed
"SABI!!!!!" In utter desperation. She could
not hear me. I ran with all my might. The
apaches fired their hellfire missles at the
pallazo. It exploded in a ball of flames.
"SABI!!!!" All there was was ruins and I
heard more helicopters in the distance. A
reconnaissance team likely of CIA
paramilitary would recon the destruction and

look for my body. They would not make the
same mistake twice. I left. I made it into the
mountains. I had a hiding place in a cave
that I would use for this purpose. I had cash
food everything I needed. Except my Sabi.
Except my soul.

Introitus from Requiem by Mozart

The word for revenge in Japanese is
Fukushuu. In ancient times revenge was
legal in japan. Vendettas had to be approved
by the authorities. Today the only authority
for revenge in japan is the Yakuza. The
Japanese mafia. There was nobody to
approve my revenge only god and my
unslakened thirst for it.
They knew I was coming. This gave them an
advantage. They could prepare for me. They
did. They had a man with my photograph
looking for me everywhere. I flew to
panama. I bought a car in cash. I took the
panamerican highway straight to the
Mexican border. I made it across the border
using my nature skills. My skills for evasion
and survival. Soon I was in the united states.

The Fatal Hour

I bought another car. I used only cash. This
is untraceable electronically. I drove to
Baltimore Maryland. There I planned my
entrance. I had to get up close. Guards were
all around the Vector building armed with
automatic weapons. They were looking for
my face. For me to appear. For me to make
my move. I was not on the surface. Posing
as the Baltimore sewage department. I
opened a manhole and I crawled beneath the
ground. I used a GPS device to guide me.
Soon I was underneath the building. Vector
personnel did not know I was there. From
this vantage I could use my wavelet detector
to look into the building. I had my laptop
and I turned the wavelets into images. They
had created an onion security system. It is a
tight circle after circle of security. You
could not just sneak in. They had snipers
placed. It was a hornets nest. I looked for a
man that had direct access to Allford Evans.
This was Henry Kawalski. The guys called
him pringle. He had an affinity for those
processed potato chips. He was delta force
alumni. He was a very formidable person.
He also had a certain facial resemblance to

me. This was important. My next step was
the key to my success.

Kyrie from Requiem by Mozart

Kabuki theater is the traditional form of
Japanese entertainment. Kabuki is composed
of three Japanese characters. Ka meaning
song. Bu meaning dance. And Ki meaning
skill.
Kabuki is performed in a special theater.
Men play all the parts. Apparently in the 17th
century women were banned from theater
because it was thought to be a corrupting
influence on the young. Displays are
overwhelming in use of color, makeup and
stylized moves. The Russian filmmaker
Eisenstein developed the modern form of
editing principles from watching kabuki.
We play many roles in life. Sometimes we
take on the roles of others. I watched and
listened. The sound of kabuki is distinctive.
It has the strings of the shamisen. Then a
variety of drums. The large odaiko and the
smaller tsuzumi and also the okawa. It is
music that is the very emanation of Japanese

tradition. First I had to develop a catalogue
of his voice. Voice is important. We
recognize people on voice alone. I practiced
his voice with great discipline. I learned his
inflections, his American dialect and his
way of pausing as he thought of what to say.
I followed him everywhere I learned his gait
and the way he held his shoulders.
Everybody was focused on Allford Evans
my universe my focus was Pringle.
One day I met him at his apartment. I came
as a UPS delivery person. I looked him in
the eye. "Henry Kawaski?"
He smiled. "Call me Pringle. Is that my
package?"
I nodded. I gave him the package. Then I
handed him a signature encoder to capture
his signature for the delivery. As he signed. I
struck him with a syringe of sionide. It
pumped a serious lethal dose into his veins.
He immediately fell to the ground in a heap.
I fished in his pockets for his apartment
keys. I lifted him over my shoulder and
carried him into his own apartment. I left his
dead body on his couch. I went to my car
and I retrieved a sewing machine and a

theatrical make-up kit. Kabuki makeup is very simple it uses the oshiroi or white face. The shade of white depends on the station in life of the character played. The mehari or red lines applied to the face and eyebrows are defining of the specific role played by the actor. My role was to play Henry Kawalski. First I made plaster of paris mold of his face. Then I filled the mold with latex. I cut the pieces of latex that I need and filled the portions where I needed body with theatrical wax. I made Kawalski's face perfect. I was him. I took his suits and I tailored them to fit me. He was my height and my weight but the suit always fits different on different people. I ate my share of Pringles in order to get his peculiar scent. The illusion I was creating had to be precise. There was no room for failure.

I clipped his identity card onto my coat pocket. I was ready to face Vector Corp. I drove his car and parked in his parking spot. I entered. His friends approached. "Did you get the porno flick I sent you?" "No." I said. "Good because I didn't send you one. But I will tonight. See ya later." I used his security card to enter the secret area of the building. I made my way up to the office of Allford Evans. There were other security consultants there with Mr. Evans. But there I was right next to the man who murdered my sweet Sabi. Ironic it was that they were looking for me everywhere except right there in Allford Evans own office.

Sequentia – Dies Irae from Requiem by Mozart

One day a swordsman spoke to cat. The
        swordsman said. 'When you are
        mushin in the
state of mind called mindlessness you act in
        unison with all nature without
        resorting to
tricks or other artificial contrivances.' The
        cat said to the swordsmen. 'We first
        must
have insight into the reason behind life and
        death. Our mind must be free of all
selfishness. That accomplished we must
        cherish no doubts, have no
        distracting thoughts;

act without calculation or deliberation. Our
      spirit must be balanced, yielding, at
      peace
with the surroundings. It allows you to be
serene and emptyminded and thus be able to
respond freely to changes taking place from
moment to moment in your environment.'
I turned to Allford Evans. He was sitting
back in his chair reading the bible. I pulled
out of my shoulder holster Pringles own
barretta pistol. Allford Evans continued to
read the bible. I said. "The trumpets of the
lord blew and the walls of Jericho came
tumbling down." He continued reading and
said. "What did you say." I pointed the
pistol at his forehead. "I said Goodnight Mr.
Evans." He looked up and I shot him in the
head at point blank range. He fell back dead.
The other two security consultants reached
for their pistols. But I moved at great speed
and shot them both in the head before they
could respond. The alarms of the building
were all sounding. I tumbled out the door
and as I became upright I shot three guards
dead. I threw the gun aside and disappeared
up a stairwell. The snipers were looking for

The Fatal Hour

me and I was looking for them. I crawled
into a duct and at the end was a sniper. I
moved slowly and silently like a cat. I pulled
out a poison dart. He looked my way and I
hit him in the shoulder with the dart. He
fainted and died. I took his weapon and his
head radio. I guided another sniper forward.
I hit him in the forehead with one shot. Then
I cleared the way by shooting all the guards
from my strategic location and confusing
them with the chatter on the radio. It was cat
and mouse and I was the cat. They used a
bounding overwatch technique to approach
my position. But I had left a recording
behind and they spent all their time focused
on my position. I was not there I was already
in the elevator. I had climbed into it from the
elevator cables on top and I was on my way
to the ground level. The doors opened and I
walked out as Pringle. I was not stopped. I
went to my car. I drove off. My victory was
almost complete. Allford Evans was dead.
But The Contract still persisted. I could have
walked away into the night. But that would
have left them as the power in the world
manipulating and killing as they pleased.

The Fatal Hour

Tearing our world asunder and leaving no
tranquility for me or anybody else.

Sequentia – Lacrimosa from Requiem by Mozart

Japanese are wed in the Shinto tradition but
they are buried in the Buddhist tradition. A
Japanese funeral happens at a crematorium.
While the dead relative is being cremated
the family and guests have a meal. Then
when the cremation is complete the relatives
pick the bones out of the ash and pass them
from one to another by means of chopsticks.
Budhist monks hold the ceremony and the
guest pays the relatives 20,000 yen and
receive a small gift in return. The urn is kept
on an altar at the families house for 35 days
and incense is burned round the clock. After
the 35 days the urn is buried in a Buddhist
cemetery. The burial of The Contract was
done by means of infiltrating CNN news
headquarters in Atlanta. I had a News
broadcast tape made privately by myself. I
rented the video equipment and had the
anchor set built by a contractor. I entered an

electronic banner that said News Alert. I worked as an production assistant. My job was to put the right digital feeds into the production console. The director would choose the feeds according to his list from the producer. I substituted my feed for theirs. The monitor came on. "A c-drive has been found in the main production console at CNN. It contains e-mails that implicate Vector corp. and the President in a secret scheme to use a single contractor for all of the national security needs..." The producer screamed. "What the hell is that!!" The director shook his head. The feed continued. "The e-mails show Vector corp and the CIA are implicated in many assassinations overseas and in this country. They operated with a license to do whatever they determined was necessary without government or the peoples oversight... More will be found as what was called The Contract is investigated....This was brought to you by the Children in war fund. 250,000 children fight in wars all across the globe..." The CNN producers found the c-drive on the production console. Nobody knows who brought it. But it destroyed Vectors stock position overnight and a President was impeached because of it. The Contract was dead and buried forever. The king is dead long live the king. Someone would try this again. Human thirst for power knows no limits. Perhaps they will not make the mistakes made by these people. Perhaps they will be smarter. But that is philosophy I am only a humble assassin.

Un Bel Di from Madama Butterfly by Puccini (Reprise)

A monk asked the master. 'What is the greatest nirvana attainable? The master answered. 'Not to commit oneself to the fate of birth and death is the greatest nirvana attainable.' Then the monk asked. 'What, then, is the fate or karma of birth and death.' The master answered. 'To desire the attainment of the greatest nirvana is the karma of birth and death.' In budhist thought it is our karma to return and seek our nirvana until we are no longer born or die. To reach the point that we remain only in

The Fatal Hour

nirvana and birth and death are only an
illusion.
I made my way back to the Caucasus. To
that horizon point where east meets west and
death meets life. My Sabi was gone. Instead
of a wedding we would have a funeral. I
visited Balkin. I would stay at his auol and
be under the care of his tiep. The noxche are
a very hospitable people. Balkin looked at
me. "I have a gift for you my friend." The
noxche were always giving their guests
gifts. It is their way. I stood their waiting in
the kitchen as Balkin went to fetch the gift. I
thought of all that my life could have been.
How Sabi must have suffered. Then I heard
the distinctive voice and the word. "Wabi."
I turned and looked and there was my
beautiful Sabi alive and breathing. I kissed
her with such profound desperation.
Apparently when the helicopters had come
balkin had taken Sabi to Tyrnyauz to do
some shopping. I married my Sabi. We have
twins. I can not tell you where we live.
So there is my story. Look, the dawn is
rising. Like Homer said in the Illiad rosy
fingered dawn. I wish you well sir. That I

The Fatal Hour

am a good man is nice to hear. You are a
good man too.
Good day sir and…..Tamam……

The Florida Brothers

The Fatal Hour

What does sky mean to you. Maybe heaven.
Maybe something blue. To me it means a
white odorless crystalline compound. A
derivative of morphine commonly known as
heroin. My name is Robert Florida. I used to
be a narcotics detective for Dade county in
Florida. Yeah my name is Florida and I live
in Florida. There are approximately 300
Florida's in Florida so take the pencil out of
your ass and join the human race. I am going
to tell you a story. Just between you and me
it goes no further than this conversation.
You may not even believe me. I was
following these goons. They were basically
selling drugs on the street. "Nice day."
Buyer says. "Beautiful sky." Seller says.
Cash is exchanged. They go on their merry
way and I follow. In my business you start at
the bottom of the food chain and move up.
These little transactions are not worth our
time on the street we want a big fish a big
bust. They were street goons but they drove
a Mercedes a sign that they were up to more
than just drugs. I followed in my shit brown
Hyundi. We ended up in a trim suburban

neighborhood of Miami. They were looking for something. There in a driveway a short bald man was quickly throwing a suitcase in the back of his Lexus. They accelerated on sight. The man jumped in his car and sped off. The chase began.

They chased the bald man and I chased them. Ring around the rosies. I informed my backup that a chase was in progress but not to interfere until I had figured out what was goin down. The best I could think was that the man had a large cache of drugs in his suitcase and these goons were the enforcers. Bingo more than a drug seller a gun toting thug for hire. We sped around for better part of an hour then the Lexus it seems ran out of gas. The bald man grabbed his suitcase and started to run on foot. The goons didn't waste anytime and shot him dead right there. They opened the suitcase and went through it but there was only clothes inside. I made my move and called back up and EMS as the goons sped off. They were apprehended up the street. I went to see the condition of the bald man. He was still alive. "You a

cop?" he said. "Yeah." "Take off my shoe."
He said.
"What?" "Take off my shoe!!!" I took off
his shoe and found a bank transaction
receipt for a lot of money maybe 2 mil. "I'm
an accountant for a bank that does not exist
but it does it handles all the money for the
drug business worldwide. Its how they
secretly move their money. There is no less
than 200 billion in the bank at one
time…you must believe me….I…I can't
breathe" At that moment he died. I stood
there in shock. At that instant the EMS
crews and more police arrived on the scene.
I put the bank transaction in my pocket
almost subconsciously, The forensics team
asked if all the evidence was clean and
untampered. I forgot to tell them about the
bank transaction slip in my pocket. My work
was over for the night so I went to pick up
my girlfriend Fern. She was a titty dancer at
the Pinnacle Club. I walked to the bar and
ordered a scotch neat. Fern smiled her long
blonde hair decorating her blue eyes.
"Looking for a bust detective." She shook
her bare breasts at me. I laughed but I stared

at my drink. "What's wrong with you
tonight was it a hard night baby." Fern said
hugging and kissing me. I just kept staring at
my drink. Fern went back to work She did
not get off until 2 am and it was only
midnight. I was deep in a trance. I pulled out
the transaction slip and looked at it.
OCCIDENTAL BANK a subsidiary of the
bank of Nairobi Kenya. $1.94 million
deposited by the Concha Corporation. The
address is the Miami international plaza. But
there is no suite number. I've been in that
building there is no Occidental bank. I paid
another visit to the Miami international
plaza that morning while my honey kept
selling her ass to high priced customers. I
entered the building and showed my badge
to the security guard. The building directory
had no Occidental bank. I asked the guard
but he said he had never heard of the bank. I
walked down the halls looking at all the
doors.
I finally counted the suites and matched
them to the directory. But that led nowhere.
I was counting the wrong things. If I were
hiding a secret bank what would I do. I

caught my hand in the elevator door. Oh shit
yes. I counted the elevators and I found one
I could not use. I asked the guard where the
elevator went. He said it was a private
elevator rumour was that the CIA had an
office here. Bingo. Occidental bank. I
picked up Fern and went home.
Next morning I met my brother at IHOP for
breakfast. John Florida my older brother was
a narcotics leutenant for dade county. He
wants his eggs just so and his toast precise
and won't get any syrup on more than one
pancake at a time. He wore the nice suits
and I wore the same blue blazer I had when I
left the police academy. "Look at this." I
said. I handed him the transaction slip. "It's
a bank transaction, for a bank that does not
exist. It is the conduit by which international
drug cartels move all their money." "How
do you know that." "Last night a man died
with this in his shoe and told me exactly
that. I'm not chasing purple rhinos. This
place is in the international plaza but hidden
behind a private elevator." My brother
turned red in the face. "You removed
evidence from a crime scene!!! Don't you

69

realize you could have internal affairs
crawling up your ass if they got wind." "I
couldn't let anyone else know." "What the
hell are you talking about." "Didn't you ever
want more. Bustin our ass getting shot at
making a measley salary while the people
we chase live the life of the rich and famous.
I want that life. I can't wait to get lucky with
the lotto. This is my chance." John shook his
head. "Why didn't you go to law school if
you wanted to get rich. Why did you
become a police officer." "Because you did
and I didn't have anything else to do." John
folded his napkin. "What are you getting
into." "Look nobody knows its there. The
guy said that no less than 200 billion sits in
the bank at one time. A good team could
break in and reallocate the funds to other
banks and nobody would be the wiser.
Under cover of an OP we could become
billionaires overnight." John shook his head
laughing. "You are a police officer and
sworn to uphold the law and you want to rob
a bank!!!" "Yeah I want to rob a bank. Its
drug money the feds would just squirrel it
away." "Your just going to throw away your

career thats what your going to do." "Look
John it does not have to be without a safety
net. We run the OP and if it leaks we still
take down the bank. We are either rich or we
are heroes either way we are looking good.
Think about it." "Don't get me involved."
"Doesn't Lori want more doesn't she
deserve more. You bust your ass for a
pension and you will either wind up a
security consultant still busting your ass and
praying you don't end up running the
register at walmart to make ends meet or
you will be in an early grave with a bullet in
your guts. That's what you want right." John
started laughing. "You are making sense and
that means we are both crazy." John lifted
his glass of orange juice. "To the Florida
brothers rich as Croesses and crazy as sin."
Conspiracies are strange animals they spread
within a tight a group but remain a secret to
the rest of humanity. Those in a conspiracy
believe themselves special by virtue that
they know something the rest of the universe
is ignorant of. They are special. They found
a secret worth keeping and that is a virtue
that gives passion to mens actions. It's the a

The Fatal Hour

church of true believers of men willing to jeopardize their serenity to a greater calling. It's a cult and the way to god is a koolaid so tasty it will make your life golden forever. We convinced a close group of narcotics operatives of our plan to steal drug money from the secret bank. Some were easy to convince others were more skeptical and took a few days of regular police work before they realized their must be a better way. They all felt that this was the chance and if they did not take it they would end up gray rats on lifes treadmill. They all had their personal reasons. Vanesa wanted to be a music diva. Sweet wanted to be owner of his own chain of electronics stores. Harry wanted to be a real estate magnate. Cujo wanted to just drink beer for the rest of eternity. We all were bound by our secret and an adventure we would never forget. We also needed a SWAT team and a group of street cops to make the operation complete. But one piece was the hardest of all and that was our computer expert Jerry. Jerry was a hacker that had been rehabilitated. "I won't do it.

The Fatal Hour

You guys are nuts. Talk to the feds go
staright and narrow and I will respect you."
"Jerry its not a crime we are stealing ill
gotten goods from criminals." I said. "I've
been to jail I'm not going back. Did my time
dude. Never again." Jerry huffed. "Look
Jerry nobody will know. Nobody knows the
place exists. Do you think the drug dealers
will call the cops on us. Their criminals for
god sake. They absorb the net loss and go
on." "What if it all gets fucked. I bet you
didn't calculate the fuck factor." Jerry pulled
down on his baseball cap. "If it gets fucked
we are doing our job we are cops they are
criminals. We are playing the right parts.
Except this time we..we…walk away with a
wad of cash if things go well." Jerry shakes
his head. "Still sounds like stealing? If you
promise I won't go back to jail." I patted
him on the shoulder. "You won't regret it
Jerry." "The girl who taught me to hack
federal computers said the same thing."
That night I picked up Fern early. She was
dancing by the pole with a large snake
wrapped round her. "We're going to be
rich."I said." She leaned over. "Are you

doing drugs?" "No. I am going to be rich and you too kitty cat." She closed one eye thinking.

"You won the Lotto." "No." "Then you are robbing a bank." "Yes." "You're just trying to get me in the sack." "Lets go home. I'll explain everything." She giggled. "Let me remove my ben wa balls and we're headed home baby." "Ben wa balls?" "Just wanted to make you jealous." She got dressed we went home. I explained the plan the team everything. Her eyes glowed like blue diamonds. She looked at me with such admiration and hunger. She smiled and her smile swallowed my soul. When we got home she said."Take out your saxophone honey I want you to play for me." I took out my saxophone. I was a fair sax player. I learned to play in highschool. Jazz is my sound my deal my way to impress chicks. Fern asked me to sit in a wing chair and play. "Blow me baby." She said. As I played she began to dance and as she danced she began to remove her clothes. "Blow a little harder baby." She said as she removed her dress. "Blow me right here baby…Yes!!!

The Fatal Hour

Like that!!!" She purred as she removed her
gartered silk stockings. She finally removed
her panties and said. "You blow me so
well." Naked as she was Fern went over to
the pizza we ordered for dinner and picked
up two pieces. She layed the pizza slices
next to her breasts. "Which pizza do you
want first." Then she leaned over and
showed me her round ripe rear. "Or would
you rather a pizza ass." She laughed. We
made love that night like carnivores at a
feast. The next morning. Fern was paging
through catalogues as I got dressed for work.
"I can buy anything I want?" she said softly.
"You can buy the moon and the Eiffel tower
if you want." She looked at me. "Can I buy a
husband." "How much." She looked into my
eyes. "For my smile." I kissed her. "Bought
and sold". I reached into my pocket. I pulled
out a cigar. I slipped off the paper cigar ring
of my Montecristo brand. I slipped in on
Fern's finger. "Until the real thing comes
along." Fern looked at her cigar ring like
one looks at dazzling diamonds.
"I think it has."

The OP had two parts. The surveillance.
Then the penetration and execution. We
leased an office suite across the street from
the International plaza. This would serve as
our control center. We set up the
surveillance tech next to the hacker tech and
paid for it all through the auspices of the
Dade county police department. It was a real
OP afterall. We were chasing drugdealers
that at least was true and having leutenant
John Florida sign off on our activities helped
immensely. It gave the project confidence at
least in the eyes of the captain and the police
chief. Sweet was the chief surveillance tech
engineer. He was the best. Harry and Cujo
were his field operatives. They placed the
bugs he manned the control room. Jerry of
coarse was our computer engineer and he
got set up with everything including a box of
corn flakes which he munched with
abandon. Vanessa we called the rocket. She
did that thing that lit mens rockets on fire.
Harry first laid a remote video chip near the
entrance of the international plaza and all
along the entrance walkway. He posed as a
window washer. As he laid the the chips he

would say "Trout one in place." The computer screen would light up with the image of the plaza entrance.

Sweet would say. "Roger that Harry the lights are clear and bright. Then Cujo entered posing as an elevator repair man. He put a video and audio chip in the elevator. "Trout four in place." "Roger Cujo theres bright lights its miller time." We studied the entrances and exits for weeks. We wanted a clear idea of who was who. Once we had gauged who the bank employees were we were ready for our next move. The bank manager was the target. His codename was the walrus. Sweet looked into the computer screen and said "Walrus on trout one launch the rocket." Vanesa wore a red wig and the tightest dress humanely feasible. Her breasts bulged and moved and when she walked the earth paused.

But her ass like some deadly wasp stung your eyes. "Rocket on its way baby." Said Vanesa. Jerry leaned over from his computer screen and saw Vanesa. "God in heaven. That should be illegal...." "Put your tongue back in your mouth Jerry." Said Sweet.

The Fatal Hour

"You want some corn flakes." Said Jerry.
"Is it fattening." "Only for you ankles."
Vanesa held papers to her belly and she
moved deliberately and crashed right in to
the walrus. The papers went flying. She bent
over to pick them up and the walrus saw her
dress inch over her tight beautiful ass. Jerry
said. "He's got a woodie or I do." Sweet
laughed. "A nice married man with a hard
on in public look how he moves his
briefcase for cover." The walrus bent down
to help vanesa. She looked in his eyes.
"Thank you…" She starred in his eyes.
"What is it" said the walrus. "Your eyes
they fill my soul." "Really." "I don't say this
to men usually but I am so attracted to you. I
hope you don't think I'm too forward." The
walrus gulped. "No you speak from your
heart that is rare." "Can I see you again."
Sweet laughed. "The trap is set bite old man
bite." "I don't know."said the walrus.
Vanesa leaned over and put her ripe bulging
breasts in his face. "I would be so grateful
like a popsicle in summer dripping from the
heat and yearning for deliverance." The
walrus was ensnared he pulled out his card

with his cell phone on it. "I'm married I
must be discrete." Jerry and Sweet gave
each other high fives. "Now what happens?"
said Jerry.
"He literally gets pumped for imformation."
Jerry looked at the image of the walrus and
zoomed in on the watch. It was a pearl faced
$12,000 rolex. "Lets buy one of these.I can
put a audio chip in it" He looked at me. "Its
one way in." "Lets hope he does not have
other watches or this will be complicated."
Said I. We successfully placed the watch on
him and we got some useful data from the
rocket. But she was angry and would not
meet him again. "If Yoda touches me again I
will barf." So there it was. The walrus wore
the watch for 2 weeks but only off and on.
We lost some data that might have been
useful. So we went with plan B. We got the
HVAC plans for the entire International
plaza. We turned off the air in mid Miami
summer. It was hot it was humid and the
bank was the only office feeling it. In we
sent Cujo and Harry to fix their air
conditioning. They laid trouts all over the
interior as well as they could. It gave us a

wide view of bank action. Phone calls and visitors, protocol and customers. It was very successful. But it had Sweet hooked on corn flakes permanenetly. Jerry also was successful. He watched the workings of the banking computers the transactions and the e-mail. He looked intricately at their failsafe mechanisms. "If you go in and storm the place like you plan the failsafe mechanism will go off and all transactions will be dumped to an emergency location. That's built into the system." Said Jerry. "How do we beat it Jerry." Said I munching on my personal box of corn flakes. "The location is overseas banks so the failsafe makes deposits and you can not beat it electronically at least from here. But if you get on the inside you can. The main frame that runs the bank is responsive only to its local network when access to failsafe mechanisms is required." John looked at me and put down his box of corn flakes. "We need to get on the inside and the only 3 people with undercover experience are Robert, Vanesa and I. So that will be our penetration crew. We go wired and hot."

The Fatal Hour

"Won't he recognize Vanesa." Vanesa took
off the red wig. Her chestnut brown hair
flowed straight and she looked similar but
different. How does she do that. "Okay I
said the new plan is set. Lets tie all loose
ends and then we rock and roll." Our
success we all attributed to the power of
corn flakes. An addiction I hold to this day.
Two days before the big day my brother
John invited Fern and I to dinner at his
home.
Lori his wife greeted us at the door. She was
immaculately dressed and coifed. While
Fern wore a t-shirt that read 'My other
boyfriend is a genius'. Lori looked at it and
looked at me and shook her head. They
showed us the baby's room with a live baby
in the crib.
It was all part of the grand tour. Fern picked
up the baby. She looked at me. She shook
her ring finger where my cigar band still lay.
I smiled. We had some champagne before
dinner. Dom perignon for our caviar dreams.
We toasted. "To the bank." And all smiled
except Lori who looked like she had just
been poisoned. We made it to dinner which

was a pot roast with carrots and mushrooms. Lori pointed out that the mushrooms were shitake and that they had medicinal value. "For we all need healing." She said. "Healing from what."I asked. "From our own actions." "You are not happy about what we're doing." She looked imperial. "None of us should be." "You think we are thieves." She began to cut the roast. "Yes I do." "What is a thief?" "Someone who steals." Answered Fern. "Lori" Fern said. "This is a fine line. Cops stealing money from criminals. You are right stealing must always be stealing no matter who does it to who. But this money is not refundable it is the product of human addiction. It is tragic money not stolen money. Who does it belong to. The addicts gave it of their free wills. No criminal forced them only the force of their physical and mental needs. The money was exploitative. It can be confiscated by the government or confiscated by the citizenry. We are the citizenry. We have equal dibbs on that money. Far better it serves us than it serves criminals or even governments. Now a days

you can't even tell the difference." Lori smiled at Fern. "You are right. I have a masters in philosophy and I ..I saw it superficially. How?" Fern giggled. "I have a masters in life." Lori laughed. "That you do." Lori poured some wine.
"To girls who can now shop at Channel." Lori and Fern hit it off so well that the next day they went shopping. They bought some Channel. Some Versace. Some Donna Karan. Nothing outrageous just enough to max out all our credit cards. The bridges were burned. Destiny was in front and we were ready.
Sargeant Nichols the SWAT leader cleaned his m-4 putting each piece meticulously together. The rifle like our plan had to be well made and calibrated in order that it could come together with precision. He looked at me. "My men are getting ready to get in position." I finished taping the wire to my abdomen." "You're the life line we count on you to be there." "We're there." I put my pistol in my ankle holster. John patted me on the shoulder. "You alright." I looked at him. "Ready when you are."

The Fatal Hour

Sargeant Rizzo called in. He was the leader of the street cops. "We are ready to close off the access when you give the go signal. I can see my bar in Acapulco. Margaritas, oysters on the half shell and me telling my great story. Get it done man. Get it done." I smiled. "We rock for you rock for us." "We'll be there." Vanesa closed the briefcase with the cash in it. There was half a million in there. It was the maximum we could get authorized for this OP. She rubbed lipstick off her teeth. "Lets kick some ass." We walked across the street carrying our cash deposit in hand. We were the Galvez brothers and Vanesa was our assistant. The rocket was armed and ready. We had made our introductions to the bank by phone and they expected us. Sweet said in our ears. "This is control all trouts clear and bright." As we entered there were Cujo and Harry mopping the floors posing as a janitorial crew. We pressed the elavator button and an intercom answered. "Occidental Bank do you have an appointment." "Yes." I said. "We are the Galvez brothers and we have a noon appointment." The elevator opened.

The Fatal Hour

We stepped in and as the elevator closed.
Harry taped red tape to the elevator door and
put an out of order sign on as Cujo cut the
elevator electricity. They laid cones all
around that read 'caution floor wet'. Cujo
spoke in our ear.
Beers on the bar. The door is closed. Happy
hunting." We were already inside. I
whispered. "Roger Cujo." Goons with
automatic weapons were all around. They
need not frisk us they they had the upper
hand and they knew it. We met the walrus.
He looked at vanesa. "Do I know you." He
said. "I don't think so." She said with
disdain. He felt it right in the soul and
moved on. "We will count the deposit and
we will be right with you." "I said. "The
banks we want the deposit to go to are right
here." I waved a piece of paper at him." He
nodded and left with the cash. A goon
watched us. The rocket made her move. She
leaned over to pick up the briefcase and her
dangerous ass blinded the guard. She looked
at him. She pulled out lipstick. Applied it.
With practiced precision she went down on
the lipstick. Once then twice. She looked at

the guard. "Do you play." The guard smiled. "I have an office right around the corner if you 'd like to step in for a moment." Sweet said in our ears. "Rocket in the corner pocket get ready to roll." Jerry laughed in our ear "That rockets strikes again." Vanesa pulled on his tie and she entered the guards office. "I said. "Rolling!!!" John and I went to the nearest computer and logged on. Jerry was guiding us in the ear for he was watching our every move from his hacker position. Helping us from his end when he could. John spoke into his mike. "Big dog are you ready." "This is big dog." Said SWAT leader. "Count off." Moving in between the ducts and the ceiling were 2 SWAT members. "Dog 1 and 2 in place." A sniper lay hidden inside an air duct. The duct opening removed and his rifle surveying the office. "Dog 3 in place." 2 more SWAT members were placing C-4 on a rear fire escape entrance. "Dog 4 and 5 in place." Big dog was hanging from a rapelling rope inside the elevator shaft with one more SWAT member at his side. His side kick smiled. "Dog 6 in place." "Big dog

in place. Lets start the party." John looked at the computer screen as I typed in the code Jerry was telling me to type. "P as in papa or T as in tango." "Tango!!"
John looked at his watch. "Close the door Rizzo." Police car lights came on and cars rushed in around the International plaza. Road blocks were laid out and all access was closed. Rizzo scratched off a list on clipboard next to a street map of Miami. "John sealed tight as a mayonnaise jar." "Roger that." Said John. I was almost finished. "Drop the corn flakes and give me the code. I can't hear you with your mouth full!" I typed furiously. We were closing down the failsafe mechanism. Suddenly Sweet at control says. "Heads up a guard is heading your way." "What do we do?" I said. "Keep typing."Said John. He pulled his shoulder pistol and shot the guard dead. Guards came running. Automatic weapons fire filled the office. John was hit in the chest and fell back. "Are we done yet!!!" I said. "No." said Jerry. "But the failsafe is coming on." Jerry typed furiously at his computer. " I blocked the switch for a

minute." "How much time." "Just type!!!" I
followed his instructions as a man with a
pistol walked up behind me. "I kept typing."
The man aimed. "I kept typing." I could feel
the man focus on the back of my head the
carbon bore aimed with deadly precision.
"Failsafe down!!!" Sweet said. "Dog 3!!!!"
The scope turned. "Not tonight darling." The
slug took down the goon. An explosion
roared. The elevator doors opened and from
all directions the tactical team guided by
control neutralized the bag guys. I went to
my brothers side. He was barely breathing.
Vanesa came running she opened his shirt.
"What are you doing I said. "I was an RN
before I became a cop." She helped all she
could. Control called EMS. Rizzo called in.
"The captain and the police chief are here
what do you want me to do." "Tell them
something just keep them off my back."
"Code 4" said Big Dog. "Alls clear let in the
ambulance only." I said holding my brother.
Rizzo told the chief and captain that the OP
was still underway and that it had developed
into a hostage situation. Authorization came
from lieutenant Florida. They nodded.

The Fatal Hour

"Yeah Florida is a good man." Jerry made all the bank transfers from across the street. We arrested the bank manager for running a drug cartel conduit. Everything worked perfectly. Our reports reflected the same story. We were the heroes that took down the biggest drug money bust in narcotics history. John recovered and was given a medal of valour. We stood there in our pressed black uniforms as they all saluted us for our extraordinary work. They even gave us a parade.

Everyone of us resigned promptly. The police morning call was an empty set. Rizzo gone the captain had to do it. "Just put up a sign he said. Temporarily undermanned. But only temporarily. Didn't Barnum say…a police man is born every second."

We sold our houses and went to the overseas banks where our money was waiting. We made our dreams come true. Rizzo opened his bar in Acapulco. He tells the story to all his customers. Big dog became a senator for the state of mississipi funded his own campaign. Harry bought real estate all over the world. Sweet became Super Sweet

The Fatal Hour

Electronics and had 1000 stores throughtout
the USA. Cujo bought a brewery need we
say more. Vanesa became a superstar named
Electra. She owns her own music company.
Lori and Fern turned shopping into their
only pass time and they did paris, new york,
Milan, and Tokyo when ever the wim struck
their fancy. Fern got a real big diamond.
But she put the cigar ring in a glass box with
a sign 'My real wedding ring.' We married
and are still very happy. John and Robert
Florida? Well they opened their own import
/ export business. 'Florida Brothers world
liquor traders inc.' We stole upwards of 20
billion dollars. It was the worlds greatest
heist. I told you you probably wouldn't
belive me.

90

www.ingramcontent.com/pod-product-compliance
Lightning Source LLC
Chambersburg PA
CBHW071340130626

46556CB00004B/1966